The Mudhole Mystery

Beverly Lewis

Beverly Lewis Books for Young Readers

PICTURE BOOKS

Annika's Secret Wish • *In Jesse's Shoes*
Just Like Mama • *What Is God Like?*
What Is Heaven Like?

THE CUL-DE-SAC KIDS

The Double Dabble Surprise
The Chicken Pox Panic
The Crazy Christmas Angel Mystery
No Grown-ups Allowed
Frog Power
The Mystery of Case D. Luc
The Stinky Sneakers Mystery
Pickle Pizza
Mailbox Mania
The Mudhole Mystery
Fiddlesticks
The Crabby Cat Caper
Tarantula Toes
Green Gravy
Backyard Bandit Mystery
Tree House Trouble
The Creepy Sleep-Over
The Great TV Turn-Off
Piggy Party
The Granny Game
Mystery Mutt
Big Bad Beans
The Upside-Down Day
The Midnight Mystery

Katie and Jake and the Haircut Mistake

www.BeverlyLewis.com

THE CUL-DE-SAC KIDS

The Mudhole Mystery

Beverly Lewis

BETHANY HOUSE PUBLISHERS
MINNEAPOLIS, MINNESOTA 55438

The Mudhole Mystery
Copyright © 1997
Beverly Lewis

Cover illustration by Paul Turnbaugh
Story illustrations by Janet Huntington

Published by Bethany House Publishers
11400 Hampshire Avenue South
Bloomington, Minnesota 55438

Bethany House Publishers is a division of
Baker Publishing Group, Grand Rapids, Michigan.

Printed in the United States of America

ISBN   978-1-55661-910-6

Library of Congress Cataloging-in-Publication Data

Lewis, Beverly.
    The mudhole mystery / Beverly Lewis.
        p.   cm. — (The cul-de-sac kids ; 10)
    Summary: Dunkum's persistence in digging out a
mysterious object that he discovers in a mudhole yields some
interesting information about previous residents in the
neighborhood.
    ISBN 1-55661-910-3
    [1. Mystery and detective stories. 2. Christian life—
Fiction.] I. Title. II. Series: Lewis, Beverly. Cul-de-sac
kids ; 10.
PZ7.L58464Mi   1996
[Fic]—dc21   96–45853
                                                                CIP
                                                                AC

For Emily,
who likes to make
muddy messes,
mostly in
Minnesota.

ABOUT THE AUTHOR

Beverly Lewis liked to dig in the dirt when she was a girl. A favorite place was the alley behind her house. Once she found an old coin from India. Another time she found a 1903 two-cent piece. "But the digging was the most fun," she says.

Now Beverly enjoys writing books for all ages. Some stories are based on her growing-up years in Pennsylvania.

Do you like to laugh out loud and solve mysteries, too? Then THE CUL-DE-SAC KIDS is the series for you!

THE CUL-DE-SAC KIDS

ONE

Splash, splish. Ooey, gooey.

Globs of mud mashed between Dunkum's fingers. He pressed his hands deep into the dirt. Digging for treasure was a great way to spend a Saturday.

Dunkum's real name was Edward Mifflin. His friends called him Dunkum. He was very tall. And the best basketball player around.

Basketball was the last thing on Dunkum's mind, today. He was dreaming of gold gems and jewels. Maybe the pirate kind.

Today was May twenty-second. A special day. His grandma's holiday book called it: Mysteries Are Marvelous Day.

Dunkum loved mysteries. Today was a good day to dig for one. Gold or jewels. Anything would do!

He really didn't know if there was gold in the hole. But it didn't matter. He loved the ooshy-gooshy feel.

What a messy, mucky hole it was—a giant one. It was the biggest mudhole in the world. Well, in the cul-de-sac.

Suddenly, Dunkum's fingers touched something slimy. Out of the goosh, he pulled a long, skinny worm.

"Maybe I should save this creepy creature for Stacy Henry. She hates worms."

"Says who?" someone called behind him.

Dunkum looked around.

Stacy was standing there, grinning.

Gulp.

"Oh, hi," he said. Dunkum tossed the

worm back into the muddy brown pudding.

Burp! The mudhole belched right there in Mr. Tressler's backyard.

"You were talking to yourself, weren't you?" Stacy asked.

Dunkum didn't answer.

"I heard you." Stacy stared at him, then at the mudhole. "What a horrible mess."

Dunkum pulled out a mound of mud. "Care for a glob of pudding?"

Stacy shook her head. "I hate dirt. Messes too."

"No kidding," Dunkum whispered. He threw the mud back into the hole. *Splat!*

"Remember Pet Day?" Dunkum said. "Remember when Jason's bullfrog landed on your lap?"

Stacy twisted her blond hair. "So what?"

Dunkum continued. "You had to go wash the froggy feel off your hands. That's

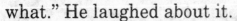

what." He laughed about it.

"It's not nice to dig up the past," Stacy said.

Dunkum stuck his hands back into the mud bubble. Deeper and deeper into the gloppy bog he pushed.

He was up to his funny bones on both arms. No one tickled his funny bone and got away with it. But something was definitely thumping his left elbow. And it wasn't a tickle. It was a bumpity-muddy-bump.

"Hey!" he hollered at the mudhole. "Quit that."

Stacy laughed at him. "Now, who are you talking to?"

"The mudhole, that's who." Dunkum hit the oozy-goozy mud again.

There was definitely something there. Something big.

Dunkum's eyes grew wide. "Hey! Maybe I've found a mystery!" He pulled and sputtered. His face turned hot purple.

Stacy stepped back. She sure didn't want to get her new outfit dirty. Or her sneakers. "What is it?" she asked.

Dunkum's eyes were slits. His lips flattened out. "A mystery in a mudhole," he whispered.

He was thinking of pirates and treasure. Maybe gold!

What *was* in the mudhole?

TWO

Dunkum stirred the mud around. He swirled and mixed it. He struggled against the hard lump.

"Maybe it's a dinosaur bone," he said.

"Cool!" Stacy said. "We could put it on display. Maybe start up a museum."

Just then the mudhole gobbled up Dunkum's arms.

Stacy yelled, "I can't see your elbows!"

Dunkum grunted and shoved. His face was down close to the mud. "The lump is too big. I need a shovel."

15

Click. Someone was opening Mr. Tressler's yard gate.

Dunkum looked up. There stood Jason Birchall. He was carrying his bullfrog, Croaker.

"Who needs a shovel?" Jason asked.

Stacy spoke up. "Dunkum thinks he found a dinosaur bone. Over there."

Jason pushed up his glasses. "Croaker doesn't see any dinosaur bones. Do you, old buddy?"

Stacy giggled. "Since when do frogs understand English?"

"Croaker does," Jason said. He knelt beside Dunkum in the mud. "Where's the bone? Is it a T-Rex T-bone?"

Dunkum shook his head. "I don't know yet. But whatever it is, it's big. Very big."

Stacy stared into the sloppy mudhole. "Icksville," she said.

Suddenly, Dunkum saw a flash of gold. His eyes bugged out. "Hey, did you see that?"

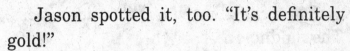

Jason spotted it, too. "It's definitely gold!"

Stacy stepped closer. Her eyes were round as quarters.

"Here, hold my frog," Jason said to Stacy.

Stacy held her hands up. "No . . . uh, not today."

"He's *not* slimy, and he doesn't bite," Jason joked.

"I know that," Stacy said.

"Here, just take him. You'll be fine," Jason said. And he handed Croaker to Stacy.

Stacy took the bullfrog. She held him far away from her body. Croaker's skin felt smooth and thin, like a balloon filled with air. She felt his lungs moving. In and out. Out and in.

Stacy shivered. She thought she was going to drop Croaker. His body felt so weird.

Then she glanced at the muddy mess. The mudhole.

Dunkum was covered with muck. Jason dived into the mudhole. Hands first.

Stacy looked at the bullfrog. Croaker's round eyes blinked back at her.

She smiled. "Frog-sitting is much better than mess-making!"

Squooshy squish, the mudhole blubbered.

Out of the spurting muddy custard came something shiny. It really *was* gold.

"Hey, we're rich!" Jason shouted.

"We aren't rich," Dunkum said. "Our treasure is stuck in the mud."

Stacy looked at the shiny gold. "Looks like a lock."

Dunkum nodded. "It's connected to something much bigger. But I don't know what."

Stacy inched closer for a better look.

Croaker blinked his froggy eyes. His

lungs breathed in and out.

Dunkum and Jason kept working. They pulled and tugged. They grunted and groaned.

"It's in there for keeps," Dunkum said. "I can't lug it out."

Jason began scooping handfuls of mud out of the hole.

When more mud was removed, the boys tried again. They jerked and yanked. They fussed and yelped.

But the mudhole wouldn't let go.

Jason was tired. He stood up all muddy.

"Well, *I'm* not quitting," Dunkum announced.

Stacy headed for the gate. "I'll get the rest of the Cul-de-sac Kids. Maybe *all* of us can pull the mystery out."

"Hurry!" Dunkum said, looking at the mudhole. "I think our gold is sinking!"

19

THREE

Something huge was in the mudhole!
Dunkum wondered, *Can it be a mummy?*

He went back to digging.

After several minutes, Jason said, "It's no use. We can't get it out." And he let go.

"Please, don't quit," Dunkum pleaded. "My fingers are slipping. I need your help."

Jason leaped back toward the hole. He grabbed on to the giant lump. He held it with all his might.

"You're pushing it down!" shouted Dunkum.

Jason crawled away. His face was caked with mud. Even his nose. He tried to brush it off. It smeared.

"Just pretend it's beef gravy," Dunkum laughed.

Jason pulled a handkerchief out of his pocket. He blew his nose. Now the handkerchief was yucky brown.

"Gross," Dunkum said.

Jason was wound up. He licked his muddy fingers. "Yummy chocolate pudding." Then he spit out the dirt.

Dunkum glared at him. "Excuse me," he said. He was still hanging on to the muddy lump. "Do you have a shovel?"

"I'll go home and check," Jason said. He stood up. Thick mud stuck to his arms and legs. It was in his hair. Splashes of mud spotted his glasses.

Dunkum scolded. "Wait till your mom sees you!"

"I'll be right back," Jason called. He ran down the street.

Dunkum was determined. He wanted the lumpy bump out of the mudhole. The lump with the gleaming *gold* object!

For a moment, he relaxed his grip and stood up. It felt good to stretch his legs. But he wasn't happy. He frowned at the mudhole.

Dunkum knew one thing for sure. He wasn't going home till the mudhole let go!

★ ★ ★

Soon, the rest of the Cul-de-sac Kids showed up.

Abby Hunter took one look at Dunkum. She shook her head. "Yuck, what a mess," she said.

"I told you it was icksville," Stacy said. She was still holding Croaker.

Abby and her little sister, Carly, stared at Dunkum. And at the mudhole.

"Does Mr. Tressler know you're

digging in his yard?" Carly asked.

Dunkum turned around. He glanced at Mr. Tressler's back porch. "I've been digging here for years."

"Well, you ought to ask first," Carly said. Her blond curls danced.

"Don't be bossy," Abby scolded.

Shawn and Jimmy Hunter ran over to the mudhole.

"We help, yes?" Shawn said. He and Jimmy were still learning English. It was hard because they were born in Korea. They were Abby and Carly's adopted brothers.

Dunkum shook his head. "I could use some serious help here. Anyone have a rope?"

"I not," Jimmy Hunter said.

Abby had an idea. "Let's make a human chain."

Eric Hagel chuckled. "Where's my camera?"

The kids laughed.

Stacy looked around. "Where'd Jason go?"

"I'm coming!" he shouted. Jason was dragging a big shovel.

"All right!" Dunkum said. "Now maybe we can solve the mudhole mystery."

FOUR

Jason came running. He plopped the shovel down and pushed it into the mud-hole.

Dunkum and Shawn clawed at the dirt with their hands. Eric and Jimmy pushed piles of mud away.

Dee Dee Winters watched as she held her cat. "Mister Whiskers wants to help, too," she said.

Suddenly, Dee Dee's cat laid eyes on Croaker. Mister Whiskers meowed and spit at the bullfrog.

"Aw, kitty, that's not nice," Dee Dee scolded.

Stacy hid Croaker under her jacket. "I guess cats and frogs don't mix," she said.

Dee Dee finally got her cat settled down. She stood beside Abby and Carly and watched the boys dig. They were making an even bigger mess.

"Wow! Look at that!" Carly shouted.

Something big was coming out of the mudhole. It was half in, half out. The mystery lump was a square box.

"What can it be?" Abby said.

"We're gonna find out!" Jason hollered.

Dunkum and Jason were still kneeling in the mudhole.

"It's almost out," Jason said.

"Let's pull the box out together," Dunkum suggested.

Abby and Carly grabbed Dunkum's arms.

"I'm ready!" Carly shouted.

"Me too," Abby said, grinning.

27

Stacy and Dee Dee decided not to help. They were trying to end a frog and cat war. Besides, they didn't want to get dirty.

Mister Whiskers kept hissing at Croaker.

Dee Dee tried to make her cat behave. She even promised him a new litter box. "Just be nice, OK?"

Mister Whiskers played dumb.

"I'll make it a *blue* litter box," Dee Dee said. "How's that?"

Meow.

Mister Whiskers was spoiled rotten.

"Show time!" Dunkum called to his friends.

Eric held on to Dunkum's belt loops.

Shawn gripped Jason's T-shirt.

Little Jimmy latched on to Shawn's back pocket.

"On the count of three, we'll lift it out," Dunkum said.

The boys hollered, "One . . . two . . . three!"

FIVE

The boys pushed and pulled. They forced and twisted.

With a mighty heave, the mudhole sneezed.

AH-AH-AAARGA-CHOOO!

Out flew a square box.

The kids fell backward. Then they saw the old chest.

"Wow!" said Abby. She crept close to the muddy chest. "There's a gold latch and lock on it."

"That's the gold we saw," Dunkum said.

He was a little disappointed because he was hoping for the real thing.

Jason rubbed his muddy hands together. "Could it be a secret treasure?"

"Let's have a look," Dunkum said.

Stacy's eyes grew big. "Can't you clean it off first?"

"Who cares about a little dirt?" Jason said. He hopped around like a rabbit.

Dunkum smeared his arm across the top of the box. "There. Now it's not so bad."

Carly shook her head. "It's still yucky."

"Maybe for you," Jason said. "Not for me." And he stood in the mud beside Dunkum, Eric, Shawn, and Jimmy.

Dunkum looked at his friends. All the Cul-de-sac Kids were gathered around. *They all want to open it*, he thought.

"I'll open the lid," Jason said. He grabbed hold of the chest before Dunkum could stop him.

"It's so-o exciting," Stacy said.

Dunkum felt his stomach flip-flop. This was *his* chest. How dare Jason just barge in like this!

Jason bent over the chest. "Is everyone dying to see what's inside?" he asked.

Dunkum could see how excited Jason was. He didn't want to be a poor sport. "Whenever you're ready," Dunkum said.

Shawn chuckled. "One . . . two . . . three!" he counted.

Jason tried to pry the chest open. His face turned two shades of pink. "Whew! It must be locked."

"Let me try," Eric said. He showed off his muscles.

The kids laughed.

Shawn counted to three again.

Eric leaned down and pulled. "Oof!"

But the lid wouldn't move.

Stacy pointed to the gold latch. "Look! It *has* to be locked."

The boys took turns observing the problem.

Dunkum jiggled the latch.

Jason poked at it.

Eric knocked with his fist.

Shawn studied the lock.

Jimmy talked Korean to it.

The lock was definitely doing its job.

"I wonder where the key might be," Stacy said.

"There's got to be a key," Dunkum added.

Eric shook the lock again. "Why would someone bury a locked chest?"

Dunkum frowned. "I wish I knew."

SIX

"We need a plan," Dunkum said.

Abby spoke up. "Let's have a meeting."

Jason jigged around. "Somebody call the meeting to order!" he announced.

"Sit down and we will," Dunkum said.

Jason plopped down on top of the muddy chest.

"Eew!" the girls shrieked.

Jason just sat there, grinning. "What's the problem?" he asked. "Mud washes off. Right?"

Stacy shook her head. "I really don't

know about you, Jason Birchall."

Dunkum whistled. "OK, we need to think of a plan. A way to open the chest."

"Hey, you forgot to call the meeting to order," Eric said.

"Abby's the club president," said Dee Dee. "Let her do it."

Abby tossed her a smile. "The meeting will come to order. Any old business?"

"Yeah," said Jason. He stuck his foot up. "I've got super muddy sneakers. Anybody worried?"

Carly and Dee Dee giggled.

"Well, at least *The Stinky Sneakers Mystery* is solved!" said Eric.

"No comment," Jason said.

"Now for the new business," Abby said. "Dunkum says we need a plan. Any ideas?"

"We should pick the lock," Carly said. "Try a toothpick or something."

"Why didn't *I* think of that?" Dunkum said.

Before anyone could say "mudhole mystery," Dunkum had dashed out the gate.

"That was quick," Dee Dee said.

And it was.

In a flash, Dunkum was back with a box of toothpicks. He tried to spring the lock. One toothpick after another snapped in half.

"The problem is the mud," Dunkum said. "It's all caked up in there."

"Let me try," Stacy said. She handed Croaker to Jason. "I'm a fixer-upper."

Abby agreed. She and Stacy were best friends. Stacy had come to her rescue many times. "Stacy has a steady hand," said Abby. "Maybe *she* can unlock the mystery chest."

The kids leaned in closer. They watched as Stacy tried the toothpick trick.

After three tries, Stacy shook her head. "I think we need a different plan."

Jason said, "Let's try a hammer."

"Smash the lock?" Abby said. "Is that a good idea?"

"We want the silly thing unlocked, don't we?" Eric asked.

"Eric's right," Jason piped up.

"Whoa," said Dunkum. "Maybe we should vote on it."

Abby called for the vote. "How many want to use the hammer method?"

Everyone voted yes. Everyone except Eric and Abby.

Jason was clapping. "Seven to two. We win!" Off he ran to his house. "Don't do anything without me," he called.

Abby went to the chest. She rubbed off some more mud. "Hey, look at this," she said. "There's writing on it."

The kids pressed against the chest. "What does it say?" they asked.

"It's hard to see," Abby said. "I think we need some soap and water."

"I'll ask Mr. Tressler about his garden

hose," Eric said. "Maybe we could use it."

Dunkum ran to Mr. Tressler's back door.

Soon, the man was outside, standing on his deck. "My, oh my. Did all of you come for a visit?" He waved his cane at the kids cheerfully.

The kids waved back.

Abby hurried across the lawn. "We hope you don't mind," she said. "Dunkum's found a mudhole he likes to dig in and—"

"There's a *hole* in my yard?" Mr. Tressler said. "Where?"

"Come, we'll show you." Abby led the old gentleman to the mudhole. Dunkum followed close behind. He was a bit worried.

Mr. Tressler leaned on his cane and looked down at the mudhole. "Well, what do you know—" His voice stopped.

Dunkum was even more worried. "I've been digging here for the longest time. Before anyone lived here."

Mr. Tressler's eyes squinted. "Well is that so?"

Dunkum thought, *Am I in trouble?*

Mr. Tressler saw the muddy chest. "Just what do we have here?"

"Just something we found," Dunkum explained.

Mr. Tressler wasn't smiling. "Looks to me like you *dug* it up. Dug it right out of my yard."

"Uh . . . yes, sir, we did," Dunkum said. He wanted to tell the old man about all the fun they'd had. About the shiny gold lock. About the old chest. But something made him stop. It was the frown on Mr. Tressler's face.

"This is *my* property," Mr. Tressler said. "You should have asked me."

Dunkum felt jittery.

"That's only good manners," Mr. Tressler explained.

Dunkum sighed. "I'm sorry about the hole. We should've talked to you first."

38

"It's too late for that," Mr. Tressler said.

Dunkum saw Jason running down the street. He was waving a hammer.

Mr. Tressler turned around, in time to see Jason. "What's that in his hand?" the man asked.

The kids stared at Dunkum.

Dunkum gulped. They were going to smash the lock on a chest. On something they'd found in a mudhole. Something that didn't belong to any of them.

Jason was out of breath. "I came as fast as I could."

Mr. Tressler turned and looked at Jason. "What's the hammer for, young man?"

Jason's eyes blinked. Fast.

Like Croaker's, thought Dunkum.

Jason looked first at Dunkum, then at Mr. Tressler. "I . . . uh . . . I . . ." Jason tried to speak.

This isn't Jason's fault, thought Dunkum. He felt sorry. Sorry and sad.

But what could Dunkum say?

SEVEN

"Digging was *my* idea," Dunkum blurted. "Not Jason's."

Mr. Tressler rubbed his pointy chin. "I see."

"Dunkum's telling the truth," Abby said.

Mr. Tressler looked at each of the Cul-de-sac Kids. "Exactly what is going on here?"

Dunkum took a deep breath. "I was playing in the mud," he began. "Something hard and big was in there. I wanted to get it out. Really bad."

Abby nodded. "That's when Stacy got all of us to come. We helped Dunkum pull out the old chest."

"Interesting," said Mr. Tressler. He tapped his cane on the ground. "Tell me more."

Abby stood beside him. "Something is written on it. Come look!"

Mr. Tressler hobbled over to the old chest.

Abby showed him where the faint letters were printed. Right on top.

"We wanted to borrow your garden hose," Jason chimed in. "So Abby could read the words."

Mr. Tressler tried to brush off the dried mud. He peered down at the dim writing. "Yes, yes. I see what you mean." He turned around and ordered Jason to get the hose.

"Yes, sir!" Jason said. And off he ran to the house.

★ ★ ★

The garden hose cleaned things right up.

The Cul-de-sac Kids took turns reading these words: *Time Capsule—Beware!*

Dunkum's heart was pounding. "We have to get the chest open." He remembered that he should ask. "Um, Mr. Tressler, is it OK with you?"

Dunkum saw a familiar twinkle in the man's eyes.

"Well now, you and your friends better get a move on," Mr. Tressler ordered.

"Yes!" Dunkum cheered.

"Double dabble good!" Abby shouted.

"Let's open the time capsule!" Jason hollered. He handed the hammer to Dunkum.

Dunkum raised the hammer high.

"Wait!" said Shawn. "We count first."

Dunkum knew what Shawn meant. "OK, you do the counting."

43

Shawn's dark eyes sparkled. "One . . . two . . . three!"

Carly and Jimmy covered their ears.

Ka-whack!

The hammer hit hard.

The lock popped.

"It's open!" Eric shouted. And he and the others pulled the lid up.

The kids crowded around. They stared into the chest.

"Wow, this is so cool," said Stacy.

"I've never seen a *real* time capsule," Dunkum said.

"What are the paper bags for?" Carly asked.

Jimmy leaned over and poked at the brown bags inside the chest.

Dunkum said, "Looks like someone wrapped up objects in lunch bags." He held little Jimmy up for a closer look.

"I never see time capsule in Korea," Jimmy said. He reached down and pulled something out. "Open up, yes?"

44

"First, Mr. Tressler should have a look," Dunkum said.

Jimmy held on to the squished-up paper bag.

Mr. Tressler leaned over and peeked, too. "What are we waiting for? Let's unwrap the loot!"

Dunkum didn't have to be told twice. "Go for it!" he said with a grin.

EIGHT

The Cul-de-sac Kids reached into the chest. They pulled out packages of different sizes and shapes. Some long and short. Some giant sized and mini.

Abby had a suggestion. "Someone should be taking notes."

"Good idea," Eric said. "But who's gonna get the paper?"

The kids looked at each other. No one seemed interested. Not with a time capsule right in front of their noses.

"Aw, forget the paper," Jason said. He

stared at the package in his hands.

Some of the kids agreed. "Yeah, forget it," they said.

Abby frowned. "Don't tell me, we have to vote about this, too?"

"No!" Dunkum said. He was sick of voting. "Somebody start opening."

"I start," said Jimmy.

RIP! He tore the old paper bag off.

Jimmy held up a cardboard tube. "Too hard to open," he said.

Mr. Tressler pulled out his pocket-knife. "Here you are, young fella. This will help."

Dunkum helped Jimmy cut open the long tube.

"Hey, check this out," Dunkum said. He unrolled a piece of paper. When it was flattened, he held it up. "It's a note."

"Read it!" Jason said.

Dunkum scanned the page. "It says, 'If you find this time capsule, it belongs to you.'"

"Hey, that's us!" Dee Dee said.

It belongs to me, thought Dunkum.

"Keep reading," Abby said.

"OK." Dunkum continued. " 'The objects in this time capsule will tell all about us.' "

"Us?" Stacy said. "Who is *us*?"

"Is the paper signed?" asked Eric.

Dunkum looked closely. "It's signed, 'The Cul-de-sac Club—CDSC.' "

"Wow," Jason said. "There must've been *other* kids living here—in the cul-de-sac!"

"Yeah, long before us," said Abby.

"Who were they?" asked Dee Dee.

"Where are they now?" said Dunkum.

Mr. Tressler waved his cane. "I have an idea," he said. "Why not open the rest of the packages? Maybe you'll find out."

"I'm next!" Jason said.

Everyone watched Jason pull out a tattered book. "Hey," he said. "It's a Sherlock Holmes mystery."

Dunkum's mouth dropped open. "You're kidding."

"Nope," said Jason. "See for yourself."

Dunkum looked at the book. "This is so weird."

"What's weird about an old book?" Abby asked.

Dunkum's face looked strange. Almost white. "I'll tell you why," he said. His voice was almost a whisper. "Because today is May the twenty-second."

"So?" Jason said.

"What's special about May the twenty-second?" Stacy asked.

Dunkum took a deep breath. "Today is Mysteries Are Marvelous Day. It's to celebrate Sir Arthur Conan Doyle's birthday," he explained.

"Who's Sir Arthur . . . whatever the rest of his name is?" Carly asked. She flipped one of her curls.

Dunkum glanced at Mr. Tressler. "*You*

50

know, don't you?" he asked the old gentleman.

Mr. Tressler nodded. "I certainly do.
You see, when I was a boy, Sherlock
Holmes was my hero. Sir Arthur Conan
Doyle wrote my favorite books. He was
born on this very day—back in 1859."

"Wow," Abby said. "No wonder
Dunkum was freaked out."

"It's mighty strange, if I do say so myself," Mr. Tressler remarked.

Dunkum couldn't believe it. Here it
was May twenty-second, and he'd found a
time capsule. And a Sherlock Holmes
book!

Some kid had lived around here long
ago. He'd loved mysteries, too. Probably
someone his age.

Where was that kid now?

NINE

Stacy unwrapped another object. It was a word puzzle book. The answers were all filled in.

Next it was Abby's turn. Then Carly's. Shawn and Eric came next. Last was Dee Dee and Dunkum.

The pile of items was growing. There was a dog collar and dish. And a Sunday school lesson.

A baseball glove, a ball, and a pack of gum. The glove was ratty. The gum was rock hard.

There were rock collections and pressed wild flowers. And dried-up gold aspen leaves.

A heavy box of green toy soldiers came next. An empty bird's nest, too.

Last of all, a tiny watch. Not gold, but pretty.

"Hey, look," Carly said. "It's the wind-up kind."

The girls looked it over curiously.

"What are we gonna do with all this stuff?" Jason asked.

Abby started to make a neat stack. Stacy helped.

"I guess we should talk to *you*, Mr. Tressler," said Dunkum. "Do you mind if we keep these things?"

The old man shook his head. "Do as you wish." He leaned on his cane. "I believe it's time for my lunch." Mr. Tressler turned toward the house.

Dunkum called to him, "Thanks for everything!"

Mr. Tressler nodded without turning around.

"Happy Mysteries Are Marvelous Day!" shouted Dunkum.

That got a smile and a wave from Mr. Tressler. "The same to you," he said.

The kids put everything back inside the time capsule. Carefully, of course.

Dunkum looked at the square black chest. "How old is this thing anyway?"

Jason didn't know.

But Eric had an idea. "Look at the Sunday school lesson. There might be a date on it."

"Good thinking," Dunkum said. He found the old lesson sheet. On the bottom of the page was a date.

Abby peeked over Dunkum's shoulder. "Wow," she said. "This thing is twenty years old!"

Twenty years? thought Dunkum. *What a long time.*

"How old would the kids be now?" asked Carly.

"Figure it out," Eric said. "Pretend they were ten when they buried this."

"Easy," said Dee Dee. "Add ten years and twenty years. That's thirty!"

Dunkum's eyes lit up. "Hey, these kids are grown-ups now!"

"They . . . they are?" Jason sputtered.

"Yep," said Abby. "And they've probably forgotten all about the time capsule."

"Maybe not," said Dunkum.

"Hey, could we track down these kids . . . er, grown-ups?" Jason asked.

Eric shook his head. "Not in a million years."

Dunkum smiled. "Anything is possible."

"With God," Abby added.

Dunkum liked Abby's way of thinking the best.

55

TEN

"What're we gonna do with the time capsule?" Eric asked.

Carly shrugged. "Aw, leave it here."

"Right here, where we found it," Dee Dee said.

We? thought Dunkum. *I found it first!*

"We'll take it to my house," Dunkum insisted.

Jason frowned. "No fair!"

"Why not?" Dunkum said. "I found it, didn't I?"

"But all of us helped pull it out," Jason

said. He stood tall and stuck out his chest.

"Jason's right," Eric said. "Let's put the time capsule in Abby's backyard. She's the president of the Cul-de-sac Kids."

Dunkum didn't want a fight. "OK. That makes sense," he said.

So Dunkum and Eric carried the time capsule down the street. Dee Dee carried Mister Whiskers. He was still hissing at Croaker, behind him.

Jason carried his frog a safe distance from the cat. The rest of the kids followed behind, like a parade. They arrived in the Hunters' backyard.

"Where should we put it?" Dunkum asked Abby.

"There," she pointed. "Under the tree."

Dunkum and Eric set the time capsule down near the swings. Beside the big tree.

"How's that?" Dunkum asked.

Abby's eyes shone. "Double dabble good."

The kids stood around. No one wanted to go home.

Dunkum walked toward the gate. "I'll be back after lunch," he called.

"Me too!" yelled Jason.

Carly asked Dee Dee to come back, too.

"Sure will," Dee Dee said.

That left Eric. He had to go to the dentist.

"I might come over later," he said. "If I feel good enough."

"What's wrong?" asked Abby. "Got a cavity?"

"Feels like it." Eric waved good-bye.

Dunkum said good-bye again. He was having a hard time leaving. He missed the time capsule already. *His* time capsule.

Everyone left, except the Hunter kids. They lived here. For a moment, Dunkum wished he lived here, too. Then he could see his time capsule any old time.

"OK, well, see you," Dunkum said.

"Alligator," Shawn said, grinning.

Abby told her brother how it went. "It's 'See you later, alligator. After a while, crocodile.' Get it?"

Shawn nodded. He laughed his high-pitched giggle.

Dunkum closed the backyard gate. He ran as fast as he could to his house next door. He thought about the time capsule. He wished it were at his house.

His dad was sitting on the front steps. He looked up from his newspaper. "Are you hungry?"

"Sure am," said Dunkum.

His dad put the newspaper away.

"Were you doing today's crossword puzzle?" asked Dunkum.

His dad nodded. "You know me well." He stuck the pencil above his ear. "Your mom's cooking hot dogs. Let's go eat."

Dunkum dashed up the steps.

"Whoa, just a minute." His dad had

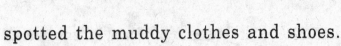

spotted the muddy clothes and shoes. Hands too. "Where have *you* been?"

"Uh, just digging," Dunkum admitted.

"In mud? Better go wash up." His dad pointed to the garden hose.

Dunkum clumped to the side of the house. This was the second time today.

When he went inside for lunch, his mom frowned. "Why must you play in the mud?"

"Don't be hard on him, dear," Dunkum's dad said. "I did the same thing when I was a kid."

"I'll go change my clothes," Dunkum offered.

"Please don't track mud!" his mom called.

"I'll be careful," Dunkum said, tiptoeing downstairs.

He headed for the washroom. Dirty clothes were piled up. Saturday was *not* their wash day.

Finally, Dunkum was cleaned up. He

headed back to the kitchen. The table was set. The hot dogs and baked beans smelled great.

His mom asked about the muddy mess. But Dunkum didn't tell much about the mystery. Or the time capsule.

His parents were grown-ups. They'd forgotten what it was like to be a kid. Dunkum was sure of it!

ELEVEN

After lunch, Dunkum's dad returned to his newspaper. Word puzzles were one of his favorite hobbies.

Dunkum's favorites were shooting hoops and digging in the mud.

Today basketball came in second. Dunkum had something else to do. He wanted to see the time capsule again.

And he had an idea. A great idea!

★ ★ ★

Dunkum hurried around to the Hunters' backyard.

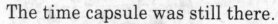

The time capsule was still there.

Abby, Shawn, and Carly Hunter had just finished lunch. They were outside looking in the chest. They pulled out many objects, looking and talking.

"We need to have another meeting," Dunkum said.

"Oh, hi, Dunkum." Abby turned around. "What's the meeting about?"

"About that." Dunkum pointed to the chest. "Let's make an exhibit."

"You mean like a museum or something?" Abby asked.

"Sure, why not?"

"Should we charge money?" Abby asked.

Dunkum walked over to the chest. "Yes. We could use the money for something special. For our club."

Jimmy was counting the rock collection in Korean.

Carly was trying on the pretty watch.

"This stuff is ancient history," said

Dunkum. "It's twenty years old, at least."

Abby nodded. "I see what you mean."

"When the rest of the kids come back, we'll decide," he said.

Abby grinned. "It's an excellent idea."

Dunkum leaned over and pulled out the old Sherlock Holmes book. "I still can't believe this was in here."

Abby asked, "How did you know about Mysteries Are Marvelous Day?"

Dunkum told her about his grandma's holiday book. "It has all kinds of special days listed."

"Like what?" Abby asked.

"Oh, let's see." Dunkum thought for a second. "There's the birthday of basketball."

"You're kidding."

"Nope."

"When is it?" Abby asked.

"January fifteenth," Dunkum replied happily. "Back in the year 1892."

"Wow," she said. "What else?"

"Children's Day is May fifth," he said. "It's a national holiday in Korea and Japan. In honor of all children."

Shawn perked up his ears. "Yes, I know that. It is true what Dunkum say."

"Your grandma's book sounds cool," Abby said.

"I'll ask her to bring it sometime," Dunkum said.

Just then Jason came in the gate. Soon, Stacy and Dee Dee were back. All the Cul-de-sac Kids were present. Except Eric.

"Let's talk about your idea," Abby said to Dunkum.

"OK," he agreed and he began to tell the kids.

"I like museums," Stacy said. "This is a terrific idea."

Dee Dee and Carly thought the idea was silly.

"Who would pay to see all this junk?" Carly asked.

"You might be surprised," Dunkum said. "And it's not junk!"

Carly twirled her hair. "I'd rather ride bikes any day."

Dee Dee didn't say much. "If it makes money, that's good, I guess."

Jason wanted to be in charge of snack food. "Who wants to help me?"

"Wait a minute," Abby said. "We haven't voted yet."

"Let's wait for Eric," Dunkum said. "We don't want him to feel left out."

So they waited. And waited.

It was almost two o'clock. Eric still wasn't back.

"Oh, well, we can vote tomorrow," Jason said.

"Tomorrow's Sunday," Abby said.

"OK, we'll vote after church," said Dunkum.

It was settled. They'd have a meeting and vote tomorrow.

Dunkum couldn't wait.

He thought about the vote. All through supper he thought about it. And during his shower.

There were five boys and four girls. One of them might be a tie-breaker.

Would his great idea fall flat?

TWELVE

After church was dinner. Dunkum had to go home and eat. So did the other kids.

There was no time for a club meeting or the vote. Dunkum had to wait a little longer.

He poked at his dinner.

"Is something wrong?" Dunkum's mother asked.

He was silent.

"Dunkum?" his dad asked.

Finally, he looked up. "Have you ever had a great idea?"

"Lots of times," said his dad.

"When you were a kid?" Dunkum asked.

"Sure." His dad chuckled. "Why do you ask?"

Dunkum sighed. "Did you ever have to wait?"

His mother frowned. "What do you mean?"

"Did your friends have to decide if it was a good idea?"

Dunkum's dad nodded his head. "Sometimes, I guess."

"Then you must've had lots of friends," Dunkum said.

"You can say that again!"

"Well, I like discovering things by myself." Dunkum was thinking about his muddy discovery. "I'm not so sure if having lots of friends is good."

His parents stopped eating. They were staring at him.

Finally, his mother spoke. "You are the

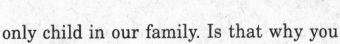

only child in our family. Is that why you feel this way?"

Dunkum nodded. "Maybe."

"Let me tell you something," his dad said. "A block full of friends can be good. Sometimes not."

Dunkum listened.

"I grew up with three brothers and two sisters," his dad explained. "We were a kid's club all by ourselves."

Dunkum scratched his head. He couldn't imagine that many in the family.

"Six kids and two parents," his dad said. "Sometimes Mom and Dad would pile us in the car. We liked to visit our uncle and aunt. They had three kids."

"That's a lot of kids all together!" Dunkum said.

His dad looked around the kitchen. "Can you imagine all of us eating here?"

Dunkum blinked his eyes. "You mean, right here? In Mom's kitchen?"

"Yep, this house belonged to Uncle Joe.

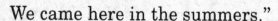

We came here in the summers."

"A long time ago?" Dunkum asked.

His mother nodded. "Your father was eight the very first summer."

Dunkum laughed. It was hard to imagine. His dad had once been a kid. Long, long ago.

★ ★ ★

Eric showed up late for the meeting. "The dentist found *two* cavities yesterday," he explained.

"Are you better now?" Abby asked.

Eric nodded. "What did I miss?"

Carly piped up. "Oh, nothing much."

Dee Dee smiled a sly grin.

Dunkum tried to ignore Dee Dee and Carly. They were being a pain.

Today he was eager. He explained his idea to *all* the kids this time.

When he was finished, Abby called for the vote. "How many want to make a display of the time capsule?" she asked.

Four hands shot up. Then one more.

"It's to raise money for our club," Jason said.

"No fair trying to get extra votes," Abby said.

Slowly, Eric and Stacy raised their hands.

But Dee Dee and Carly kept theirs down. Without them, the vote had passed.

Abby cheered. So did Dunkum and Jason.

"We're gonna have the best time capsule exhibit ever!" Dunkum said.

★ ★ ★

Six days later, everything was ready.

The display was the hottest thing around!

Kids from Blossom Hill School came. So did cousins of the Cul-de-sac Kids. Lots of parents came, too.

Stacy showed her mom the old watch. And the Sunday school lesson.

Shawn and Jimmy showed their parents the rock collection. Abby and Carly showed the crushed wild flowers.

Dunkum's parents seemed to enjoy themselves, too.

"What a wonderful idea, son," Dunkum's dad said.

"Thanks."

Suddenly, his dad stopped. Right in front of the giant word puzzle book.

"What's wrong?" Dunkum asked.

His dad picked up the book and looked inside. He began to laugh. "This is *my* writing!"

"Yours?" Dunkum said. "How could that be?"

"Where did you find this stuff?" his dad asked.

"In Mr. Tressler's backyard."

Dunkum's father nodded his head, laughing. "Well, that makes sense."

Dunkum was confused. "Are you saying *you* buried the time capsule?"

"My brothers and cousins buried it. And so did I." He grinned at Dunkum. "It was one of my great ideas."

Dunkum couldn't wait to tell his friends. He ran around the exhibit telling them. Mr. Tressler, too.

"What about the Sherlock Holmes book?" Mr. Tressler asked. "Did it belong to your father?"

"I'll ask," Dunkum said.

He found his dad counting the rock collection. Jimmy Hunter was counting, too. In Korean.

"What other stuff is yours?" Dunkum asked his dad.

"The crossword puzzle book and this." He pointed to the colorful rocks.

"What about the rest?" Dunkum asked.

His dad had to think. "The baseball glove was Uncle Joe's. He never knew what happened to it. The rest of the stuff belonged to my cousins and brothers."

"Not your sisters?" Dunkum asked.

"You know how some girls are about a great idea," he said. "Mostly a muddy one."

Dunkum understood.

He glanced at Dee Dee and Carly across the yard. They'd voted against him. Now they were helping Jason at the snack table.

Dunkum thought, *I'll invite them to make mud pies tomorrow.*

And that's what he did.

THE CUL-DE-SAC KIDS SERIES
Don't miss #11!

FIDDLESTICKS

It's soccer season for the Blossom Hill Blitzers. Shawn Hunter is much smaller than the other boys, but he's speedy. And he's dying to make the team.

Some of the kids call him "Fiddlesticks" because he brings his violin to after-school practice. And because his legs are "skinny as sticks."

Secretly, Shawn works out at home, trying to develop a few muscles. He weighs and measures himself every day for two weeks. The Cul-de-sac Kids help, too.

Can Shawn possibly make the team? Or will steady teasing at school mess him up during tryouts?